CHIP BOY
Jillian Powell

Contents

The arrival

"What is he called?" Mum asked.

"Don't know. It begins with Z, I think."

"Z? Zack?"

Joe shook his head.

"Well, where is he from then? Is he French?"

"I don't know."

"Well, we will soon find out," Mum said. "Here's the minibus now. Please be nice, Joe. He will feel strange away from home."

Joe didn't answer. He didn't want anyone staying with them.

Joe's teacher got out first. Then the children began getting out. The teacher read out a list of names.

One by one the children found their host families.

There was only one child left.

"Oh, and Zeb," Joe's teacher said. "You are staying with Joe and his family."

"He looks nice," Mum said.

More like weird, Joe thought.

"This is my room," Joe said. "You can sleep there."

He pointed to the bottom bunk.

"That's good!" Zeb said.

"You can plug the light in there," Joe said. "In case you want to read in bed. I am reading this."

Joe showed Zeb his sci-fi book.

There was an alien on the front. His head looked like a rugby ball.

"Ha, ha!" Zeb said. "Who thinks we look like that?"

"No, that's the alien you dork," Joe said. "It's quite good. You can read it if you like."

"I would rather read about humans!" Zeb said.

"Yeah, right." Zeb really was weird, Joe thought. Now he was unplugging the light.

Zeb sat down on the bed.
"Soon time for chips!" he said.

"Chips? You want some chips?"
Joe asked. "We can ask mum, but
sometimes she says no chips!"

Zeb looked unhappy.
"For me, chips every day."

"Right," Joe said. And Mum said **he** was
chip mad. Still, if they got chips
every day, that wouldn't be so bad.

"These are my computer games," Joe said. "Want to play one?"

Zeb shook his head.
He pointed at a jigsaw.

"Oh that's really boring," Joe said. "It's planet earth. It's quite hard too."

But Zeb shook out the jigsaw.

"Best to start with the black bits," Joe said. "They go round the outside."

But Zeb had already started. He worked faster than Joe had ever seen. In a flash, the jigsaw was done.

"Wow, that was quick!" Joe said. "Hey, Zeb. You can show me where you live. Is it here?"

Zeb shook his head.

"Here, then?"

Zeb shook his head again.
"I live there!" he said.

Just then, Joe's door opened.

"The chips are ready, boys!" Mum said.

"Time for chips!" Zeb said.

But Joe was staring at the jigsaw. Zeb had pointed to the black bits. And that was outer space.

Stranger still

That night, Joe lay awake. He kept thinking about Zeb and the jigsaw.

And that wasn't all. They had eaten chips for tea. But at bedtime, Zeb said again, "Soon be time for chips!"

"You can't have chips for breakfast!" Joe said.

"Mum won't let us. I did try asking once!"

There was no answer. Zeb must have been asleep in the bunk below.

Joe read a bit more of his sci-fi book.

He was nearly at the end. He would finish it tomorrow. He closed the book and turned off his light. Then it hit him.

Zeb had said, "Who thinks we look like
that?"

Joe turned on the light again and looked
at the book. He began to shake.

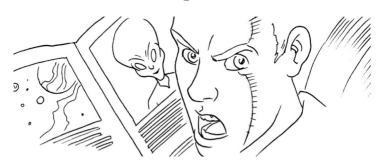

There was an alien sleeping in the bunk
below him!

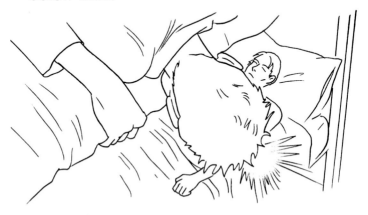

Joe looked down. It wasn't quite dark.
There was a soft green light.

Something was plugged in. Joe looked harder.

Zeb was sleeping. A tiny green light was blinking by the plug. And there was another tiny green light blinking in Zeb's arm.

There was no mistake.
Zeb was plugged in.

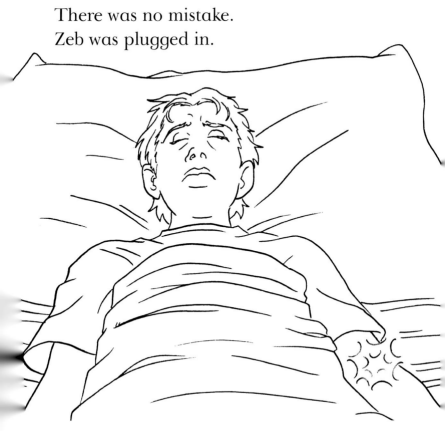

The eyes have it

The next day, Joe's class had a day out.

"We are going to see a show," Joe told Zeb. "It's called the Sky at Night. It's all about the stars and planets."

He nearly said, "So you can show me where you live."

He looked at Zeb. But Zeb was saying nothing.

On the bus, Martin Hills began
making trouble.

"Hey, Joe. Where's your friend from?"
Joe didn't answer.

"Is he from LOSER land, like you?"

Loser yourself, Joe thought.

He made sure they sat away from
Martin for the show.

It soon began. Stars and planets came up on a big screen. Their names boomed out.

Pluto, Mars, then a name Joe had never heard before. At that name, Zeb began to twitch.

Joe looked round. Zeb was staring at the screen. His eyes were glowing green.

They looked like a cat's eyes at night.

"Are you okay?" Joe asked.

"Need chips!" Zeb said. He took something out of his bag. It looked like an MP3 player.

He put the buds in his ears. Joe saw a green light blinking.

So that's it, Joe thought. That's where you come from.

Alien powers

"So which planet are you from, Joe?"
It was Martin Hills again.

"Is it Planet Stupid?" Hills and his
mates laughed.

"I said, is it..?"

"I heard you.
Very funny, Martin,"
Joe said. He didn't
turn round.

Then something hit him.
Martin was throwing crisps at him.

Joe still didn't turn round. Perhaps
Martin would get bored.

Then something funny happened. Zeb put his hand up. He looked like a policeman stopping the traffic.

A crisp hung in mid-air. Then it turned round. It flew straight back at Martin.

It happened again, and again. Martin was covered in crisps.

"Who's doing that?" Martin shouted.
The crisps seemed to multiply. Martin
Hills was being attacked by a bag
of crisps.

Joe had never seen anything so funny.

But his class teacher had heard the noise.
He was coming down the bus.

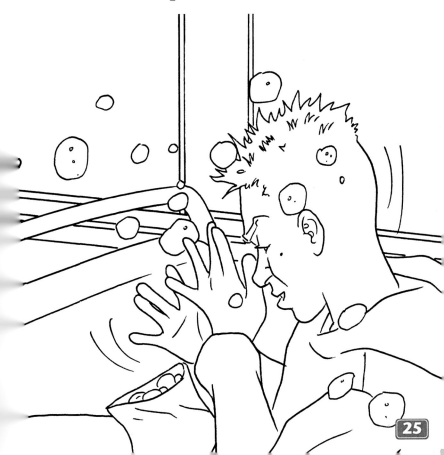

"Hills!" he shouted. "What's this mess?
Why are there crisps everywhere?
Give me that bag! You will be staying
on the bus for our next visit."

Martin handed over the bag of crisps.
He looked like he was afraid of them.

"How did you do that?" Joe asked Zeb.

Zeb held up his hand.
"Chips!" he said simply.

"So can you do anything with chips?"
Joe asked Zeb.
They were back in Joe's bedroom.

Zeb nodded. He held up his hand. He
looked as if he was washing a window.
A screen appeared in mid-air.

"That's so cool!" Joe said.
"What's that?" He pointed at the
screen.

"That's my planet," Zeb told him.
"That's where I come from."

"Cool!" Joe said again.

"Want to play the jigsaw game?" Zeb
asked him. He moved his hand again.

The screen broke up like a jigsaw.

"Wow!" Joe said.
He grabbed a bit of a big yellow planet.

Slowly, another world began to form in
front of him.

Mum was in the kitchen. She was reading something.

"Oh, Joe. There you are," she said.

"What are you reading?" Joe said.

"It's from the school," Mum said. "They are really pleased everything went so well. They are planning the return visits already."

"You mean, Zeb might come to stay again?" Joe asked mum. He had missed Zeb since he left. They had so much fun with chips and Martin Hills.

Since then, Martin had stopped
bullying him. He had a lot to thank
Zeb for.

"No, not this time," Mum told Joe. "It's
your turn to do the travelling!"

"You mean?" Joe's mind was racing.

"Yes. This time, it will be your turn to stay with Zeb," Mum said.
"He says he will be really happy to show you around."

Joe gulped.

"We will have to get you a passport, in time for next summer," Mum said.

Do you need passports for outer space? Joe wondered. Mum didn't know what she was saying, but he was going to stay with Zeb on another planet.

SPACE PASSPORT